Age of Gaia

Renwick Russell

SERENDIPITY

Copyright © Renwick Russell 2006

First published in 2006 by

Serendipity
First Floor
37 / 39 Victoria Road
Darlington
DL1 5SF

British Library Cataloguing-in-Publication data
A catalogue record for this book is available from the British Library

ISBN 1-84394-199-6

To my wife Jean

ACKNOWLEDGEMENTS

The Tran's song in chapter 12 is taken from the Sri Atma Gita

Age of Gaia

1

Mindful immediately of the significance of the day, Zero sat bolt upright in bed, instantly wide awake. He was full of calm, coherent energy, his mind stilled and made powerful by the awareness that today heralded the start of a period of great personal evolution, perhaps even escape from the grip of Gaia.

He remained in a state of bliss while his body dressed itself rapidly and rushed down the stairs, to be greeted by his mother proffering an earthenware bowl filled with rice. He started to eat greedily, without attention, and immediately (even more sharply than usual) experienced Gaia's rebuke. His face displayed the habitual grimace, and he silenced himself inwardly for a moment of gratitude, and ate the remainder of his breakfast with the long-practised reverential attitude which would ensure no more Gaia-pain. He kissed his mother and hugged her, knowing that he wouldn't see her again for several months then grabbed his coat, flew through the door and mounted his bicycle in what felt like one fluid movement.

The journey to The Academy was a real joy, whistling down the streets and savouring the early morning sunshine. He was of course aware that he was something of a focus of attention, and he was delighted to hear his new nickname whispered as he passed. "There goes Zero the Hero" muttered one of his former classmates, his jealousy thinly disguised as distaste. "This time next week he'll be telling us common souls what to think".

Zero paused for a while at a cross-roads, and studied a Tran as he settled down in the lotus position. Zero always felt that the Trans' apparent disregard for all things material was a little too contrived, and he watched this one settle himself down amongst the surrounding squalor in a position that was perfect in its apparent randomness. Zero had always wondered why you never saw Trans at Chrislamic ceremonies, and why it was they chose to worship Botu. The people around the Tran went about their business, their faces marked by the strain of years of Gaia-torture, and he had a flash of empathy with those who chose to give their lives in the service of the Commoners.

No time for conjecture, he hurtled round the cobbled streets leading to The Academy and was delighted to see Thomas sitting on the steps waiting for him. They rushed towards each other and embraced. This was the moment, the fulfilment of all their desires. No dream inspired by the exuberant optimism of youth could exceed this - to be accepted by The Academy, with a handful of others who would one day form The Elite, was more than either had dared to hope for, but for them both to be accepted, for them to be allowed to be together in this highest of callings, was bliss beyond imagining. Even from the steps they could feel the powerful atmosphere of The Academy which seemed to lure them in, irresistible but simultaneously curiously disturbing. All that was great in humanity, all that separated him from the lower species, the intensity of spirit and depth of knowledge and understanding was here, behind the Doric columns and enclosed in some strange way by the old stone walls before them. As the bell rang and they slowly traversed the steps together, they experienced a sense of timelessness, of slotting into something greater and more profound then they had ever sensed before.

Ushered into a classroom by a green belted Elite member, they were delighted to find that there seemed to be no predesignated seating arrangement, and they quickly found seats next to each other. An elderly, black belted man, bright eyed and bald headed introduced himself as Paul, who was to be their teacher. He was everything they had imagined, almost a characature of a monk, his palpable friendliness and wisdom underlined by the ethereal quality of his pristine white robes. He smiled and welcomed them all.

"We're going to start with a little test, which we've found over the centuries has formed a good introduction to life here at the academy. You have all been selected as the most able members of your generation, and you should have nothing to fear. It's partly for your own benefit, as it will give you some insight into your own intellectual strengths and weaknesses, and it helps us to know which areas of your development most need work."

All the students had been through countless examinations, and they were all extremely bright. Most had learned to enjoy tests, and the atmosphere was one of eager anticipation as Paul handed round the sheets. When every pupil had a pile of pieces of clean white paper on one side of his desk, and the test paper turned upside down on the other, Paul told them all to turn over the examination sheets and start work. Zero quickly picked up the sheet and gasped as he realised what he was being asked to do. Across the top of the paper was written quite simply "Academy Examination 0/1". The rest of the sheet contained only one straightforward question, but he had to fight to prevent his mind from panicking as he realised for the first time in his life that he had no idea how to begin to answer the question. At

School, he had excelled at both arts and sciences, like all the other successful Academy applicants, but he now realised that he had graduated to a completely different level of study. The four words on the paper in front of him seemed to loom towards him as he struggled to regain the clarity of mind which had set him apart from his former classmates. The question simply read "Write all you know".

2

As his mind started to lose concentration, it was Thomas who jolted him back into a calmer state. He could hear Thomas writing furiously, and he knew that Thomas's extraordinarily ordered and logical mind would be hard at work, classifying and sub-classifying, setting out the knowledge he had gained at school in a masterly summary in the five or six pages available to him. Zero knew that Thomas was in his element with this sort of approach, but he also knew that his own strengths lay elsewhere, for he had a unique ability to find the overview, to transcend the problem and find a different level, and he could sense that the question could suit him as well as Thomas. In a flash of intuitive inspiration which had become his intellectual trademark, he remembered a line from Keats which had moved him deeply, and he felt contained great truth. He picked up the pen, wrote his name at the top of the page and answered the question, all in a few seconds. He suddenly realised that he was filled with a sense of smug self-satisfaction and braced himself for the Gaia-pain but to his absolute astonishment there was no rebuke. Reeling from this, he stood up and handed the paper to Paul, completely puzzled by the event. He left the room and sat on the steps outside to wait for Thomas. Could it really be that the atmosphere in The Academy was strong enough to form a barrier to Gaia's influence? Did his acceptance to The Academy signify the end of Gaia's hold over him?

Inside Paul picked up Zero's answer and smiled as he read it. "Beauty is Truth, Truth Beauty. That is all you know in life, and all you need to know." Certainly it wasn't original, but it was still one of the best answers to The Academy's first test he has read in thirty years of teaching. It reminded him a little of his own answer to the Philosophy question he had wrestled with in his own student days so many years ago - to the question "Is this a question?", he had answered "If that is a question, this is an answer!" for which he had been granted the class prize for the year. He knew that he had an exceptional pupil in Zero and his friend Thomas also had something about him, and Paul's spirits lifted as he contemplated the prospect of the next year with his new class.

Meanwhile on the academy steps the two friends were excitedly comparing notes on their first experience of academy life. Thomas laughed out loud when he heard Zero's answer.

"Jehallah!" he exclaimed, "you've always been a chancer!"

They spent some time discussing their next class. Thomas in particular had always been interested in history, and they had been told that they would be studying the foundations of Chrislam. They also knew that this was somehow connected with the dawn of the Age of Gaia, but such subjects were only taught to the privileged few who graduated to The Academy, so their discussions were only based on conjecture and superstition.

An hour or so later, sitting in class, they could hardly wait to hear what Paul had to say. He talked at some length about early twenty-first century politics, and about the warring religions of Islam and Christianity. In the pre- Gaia period, people had been free to commit appalling acts of selfishness and degradation which were so shocking to the students that they quickly realised why such information wasn't made freely available to commoners. The Islamic world was plagued by violence and hatred of Christians, and the Christian culture had descended to an appallingly shallow and self serving level, riddled with greed and debauchery.

"What I don't understand is how, with all this mutual hatred, the two factions were ever persuaded to combine under one religion," Thomas was asking.

"Strangely enough, it all eventually came down to politics, and the saving of face," Paul explained. "Both sides knew that if they continued at each others throats, civilisation would be destroyed, so there was an unspoken understanding that the war had to end. The problem was to allow each side to convince their followers that they had won. The religious differences were resolved by allowing different forms of Chrislamic worship in different parts of the world, but the sticking point eventually was the semantic issue of what to call the hybrid religion. It was the genius of one man, His Holiness The Right Honourable Sir Anthony Blair, the first World President, which possibly saved the entire human race. He above all others realised that it was presentation which was all important, and came up with the "Chrislam" solution. He convinced the Islamic scholars that their religion was the only one of the two which was entirely represented in the name, and that the Christians had tacitly surrendered the superior position by allowing the name of their religion to be shortened while the name of "Islam" was kept in its entirety. Meanwhile the Christians were pacified by the fact that their name came first. You have to remember that these were relatively primitive times, and that the freedom allowed these people without the guiding hand of Gaia had led them into a petty existence. They were, by our standards, lost souls, and their leaders were no better than their commoners."

The two boys left their class in a sombre mood, struggling to get to grips with a world long ago in which Gaia did not hold sway, and in which people were free to be entirely selfish. A lifetime of remembering to cultivate a reverential attitude towards Gaia, or else suffer the pain of Gaia's rebuke, made it hard for them to contemplate the life which had been led by their predecessors. At the same time, their appetite for knowledge which had always been strong, had been made even sharper, and they couldn't wait for the next few weeks at The Academy where they knew they would start to unravel the mystery of the dawn of the Age of Gaia.

3

Keeping up with the rate at which they were now being taught was a problem sometimes, but it was amazing how quickly the two friends and their classmates adjusted to life at The Academy. Their lives at their previous schools had by now become something of a dream, although Zero often found himself thinking about his friend Unity.

They had been together at school for some time before Zero plucked up the courage to talk to her. He had always been fascinated by her and loved to listen to her talk, which was pretty much her favourite occupation. She was small, barely taller than five foot, with a lively animated manner. What really fascinated Zero, though, was her eyes, which sparkled when she spoke in a way which evoked the Elven people from the tales his mother used to read him when he was very young. She had never really paid him much attention until the time their maths professor had talked about number theory for the first time.

"Most numbers are of no philosophical importance, being merely generated by the simple expedient of adding one to the previous number. The only numbers of any real interest to the mathematician are Zero and Unity, from which all other numbers can be easily derived." He paused at this point to smile meaningfully at his two pupils, while the rest of the class snickered quietly in the way of schoolchildren. Unity had taken the opportunity to turn and look at Zero in a way which had made him freeze completely. She seemed to look right inside him, as if she could see some hidden depths in him of which he was unaware, and it seemed to him that the whole universe was contained in that moment.. When she turned away, with a wry smile, it was as if he had fallen from grace, back to a reality which he had previously regarded as normal, but which now felt dull, lifeless and uninteresting.

To Zero's delight they had become friends after that, with Zero spending more and more time with her and less with Thomas, until the time when they had had to choose the next stage in their paths through life. Zero had always known that his destiny lay at The Academy, and he was devastated when Unity declared that she wanted to go into Commoner Service. She was easily bright enough for The Academy, and sometimes scored more highly than Thomas and Zero in schoolwork, but she had no doubt that the Academic route was not for her.

There was little time to think of the past, though, and so much to take in. Since he had started to live at The Academy he had no experience of Gaia pain and his classmates confirmed that they had the same experience. Neither were there any Chrislamic ceremonies. The monks were a little inscrutable when quizzed about this but explained that they would understand everything in good time. Both Zero and Thomas excelled at their tests and rose to the top of the class. The only fly in the ointment was that there were so many questions left unanswered, and the more they learned, the more they realised they didn't know. It felt like they were growing in ignorance rather than in knowledge, although they had managed to piece together some knowledge of the structure of the Elite. There was a President, a somewhat elderly man by the name of Seven who lived at one of the other four Academies in the world, and then a hierarchy of monks distinguished by different coloured belts, from the green of novice monks to the black of the most experienced, through blue, orange and red. Only the black belted monks were allowed to teach, and Zero was particularly fond of Paul, who had become a mentor and role model as well as a teacher. He was therefore very disappointed when Paul announced one day that it was time for their class to be taken over by another teacher. Their history studies hadn't progressed a great deal, which frustrated Zero and Thomas because they were desperate to find out more about the dawn of the Age of Gaia, but they had been told that in order to understand what had happened, they would have to learn more about Consciousness, which Paul explained was not his field.

It was a rather bleak Tuesday afternoon when they filed into their new classroom to await their new teacher. When he entered the room, there was a gasp of surprise from the entire class. The teacher, a tall thin man with an unkept beard and a thick mass of long hair, closed the door, crossed the room with long purposeful strides and sat cross-legged on the desk. The teacher was a Tran.

4

Everyone in the class was taken totally by surprise.

"By the beard of Jehallah, I was not expecting this!" Thomas whispered to his friend. "I didn't even know they could speak!"

The class settled down and waited for the Tran to speak. And waited. Then they waited some more. The Tran simply sat there, smiling benignly and looking into the middle distance. Everyone felt increasingly awkward, but no-one dared to talk or even whisper. The atmosphere in the room became increasingly tense and Zero could see all the other class members fidgeting. Alice, a dark skinned girl who was nervous at the best of times, was playing energetically with her pen, and Sebastian, a rather quiet and thoughtful student was doodling abstractedly on the front of his notebook. Eventually, the Tran spoke.

"Why are you so nervous?"

The tone of his voice clearly implied the rhetorical nature of the question, and anyway everyone was too unsure of their new teacher to formulate a reply. Fortunately, after another awkward pause, the Tran continued. His speech was slow, quiet and pleasing, with a melodic feel and as he spoke Zero could feel himself relaxing more and more.

"Do you fear the pain of Gaia?"

Another rhetorical question, followed by another pause. Thomas smiled quietly to himself, as it occurred to him that he could probably summarise an entire year's lecture course by this guy on the back of an envelope. At least revision wasn't going to be a problem.

"No, you fear yourselves. You sit without stimulation and you feel uncomfortable. Ask yourselves why this is."

Another pause, longer this time. Zero was completely hooked now, every particle of his being was now focused on the strange looking man sitting cross legged on the desk in front of him. He realised that the sense of relaxation was a palpable thing, not just a mood, and that it was emanating from his new teacher. He was also beginning to feel a little strange, though, as if he wasn't really there, and yet at the same time he felt more focused and alert than he had ever done in his whole life. The teacher continued, in his slow and steady way.

"You are here to learn about consciousness, about who you really are. If you fail to learn this, and yet learn everything else about the world and how it works, you will know nothing."

This time, once he had stopped talking, he went round the room with his eyes, looking deep into the eyes of each member of the class. It seemed to Zero that the Tran didn't look for long at anyone, and yet when it came to his turn he felt that it took an eternity before the teacher moved on. It was an experience of time standing still, and a sense of an enormous energy, as if he had spent his life as a children's toy which had been powered by weak batteries, and someone had just plugged him into the mains. Afterwards, he was to discover that every member of the class had experienced the teacher looking at them for much longer than the rest.

When the teacher had finished, or at least after his customary pause, he uncrossed his legs, and strode towards the door. With a shock, Zero realised that an entire hour had passed and the lesson was now over. Just as he was wondering what he was supposed to have learned, the Tran turned, with one hand on the door, and said "On my desk is a pile of documents. The Academy has written notes for this course. That is the first chapter. Read it."

And he was gone, leaving the class almost gasping with a mixture of relief and confusion. Suddenly, a thousand questions sprang to Zero's mind, and he realised that the spell cast by the Tran was over. Only now did he realise how peaceful his whole being had become in the presence of the Tran, but he was back to normal, his mind running more quickly but the sense of enormous energy had left the room with his teacher, and he was back to running on batteries again. He joined the jostling horde of pupils struggling to get their printed notes, and left the class silently, pausing outside to take in the cool afternoon air.

5

Until now, there had been very little written material issued by the Academy so Zero's curiosity was aroused as he picked up the small brochure which he had collected from the Tran's class. He studied the front cover and smiled. On the front page was a picture of the front of The Academy with its steps and pillars, and overlayed on this image was the title in large black print:

Academy Consciousness Course

What amused him, though, was the smaller subtitle below:

Who am I?

What is Life?

(and other dumb questions)

He turned over the page and started to read.

Chapter One

Before we launch into the core questions "Who am I?" and "What is Life?" so lambasted on the front cover of this course, we have to address the question of consciousness.

Just addressing a question like "what is consciousness?" has a very interesting effect, which the student may well have noticed. Our minds simply don't like to be asked such questions. A strange and uncomfortable haziness tends to descend over us. The internal dialogue tends to run along the following lines:

Q. What is consciousness?

A. Ummmm. Memory of being asked question by unpopular Geography teacher famous for sadistic use of sarcasm targeted at less able pupils and knowing that the answer depends on knowledge gained from homework which for some very good reason you didn't do. Ummmm (more uncomfortable silence). Flood of amazingly creative ideas for what to do with the rest of the day combined with an almost unnatural level of energy required to do them.

As it happens, I know why you think you don't like to answer such questions. It's because you think you are stupid.

I have more news for you on that front. You are.

Before you embark on a tirade of righteous indignation and start invoking your doubtless excellent school results and proficiency in needlework to refute my outrageous allegation, perhaps first I should explain how it is that I know you are stupid.

Its because you are (almost certainly) a member of homo sapiens, the self-proclaimed pinnacle of evolution, and we homo sapiens are all stupid. As the 20th century physicist Einstein famously said, "Two things are infinite – the universe and human stupidity, and I'm not sure about the universe." (If you're not a member of homo sapiens, welcome to planet Earth, and the answer to the question which has no doubt been troubling you is that Cricket is a sport, enjoyed by millions of people, a surprisingly large minority of whom are both awake and facing the right direction.)

However I would submit that the rather surprising truth is that your stupidity is not the reason you have trouble thinking about consciousness. There are two problems in this regard which have to be addressed.

Firstly, the intellectually inclined among you will be gagging for a definition of "consciousness", and I'm not going to give you one. This is not because of any contrariness on my part, but rather because consciousness in the sense that I mean it, cannot be defined. By consciousness, I mean who you are when you aren't thinking or feeling. You may well have had the experience of this kind of pure consciousness when meditating or walking in the hills (or any other activity which enables you to transcend thoughts and emotions). Consciousness is who you are on a much deeper level than your thoughts and emotions. The reason it cannot be defined is that definition exists on the level of the intellect, and consciousness exists on a level beyond that of the intellect. Consciousness is Dylan Thomas's "Force that through the green fuse drives the flower".

For the pedantic amongst you, please note that "consciousness is who you are when you aren't thinking or feeling" is not a definition, but rather an indication of what I mean. I have to assume that you the reader are with me up to this point, and if you're not you may as well rethink your career at The Academy.

The second problem, and the main reason you have trouble thinking about consciousness is that your mind is pointing the wrong way. This, more than stupidity, is the real issue. The human mind has evolved over countless millennia to enable us to deal with problems posed to us coming from the environment through our senses. Consciousness is that which flows through the mind and the mind cannot see it directly.

For this reason, and since consciousness is the basis for centuries of rather unclear philosophical debate it is plainly no easy subject to consider. Fortunately at this juncture I have some very good news. Cast your mind back to school, when your maths master announced an unexpected test on a tricky area of algebra or geometry. Recall that fear in the pit of your stomach, and the elation which followed when it was revealed to you that it was a multiple choice test. Imagine now that each question only has three possible answers. Blindfolded with a pin you can get 33%! Even with your somewhat sketchy understanding of the subject, 70 – 80% seems easily achievable and you can launch into the test with something approaching enthusiasm.

There follows a multiple choice question about consciousness, which perhaps more than any other question defines how you see yourself and the world. Please take some time over the question and not just give the first answer that pops into your head.

The question is as follows:

How many consciousnesses are there in the universe?

As promised, the question is of the multiple choice variety, and the possible answers are:

A) 0
B) 1
C) >1

Please consider your answer for the next lesson.

Zero put the pamphlet down. He loved the chatty, almost jaunty style, but his head was swimming with the enormity of the issues raised in a couple of short pages. If this was the beginning of the course, was he going to make it to the end? For the first time in his life, he doubted his ability to cope with the task set to him. How was he supposed to know how many consciousnesses there were in the universe? Or was the question as easy as it looked? Surely, since there was Gaia, and there was himself and all the people he had met in his young life, the answer must be C. Intuitively he knew that there was more to this question than he realised, but he also knew he wasn't going to make any progress without a good night's sleep.

He slept fitfully, though, anxious about his lesson the next morning. Was he really about to learn the answer to what had once been called Life, The Universe and Everything?

6

Prayers were being held throughout the country, and in the hospital the morning attunement was just starting. The doctors, nurses and trainees were all gathered in the Great Hall in a circle, holding hands.

"We are all One under Gaia"

They chanted together as they always did.

"Love One Another
  Serve One Another
  Remember Gaia and Jehallah"

Kindergarten mantras. Unity wondered how meaningful it was to repeat the same liturgy every weekday morning from pre-school until retirement. If you asked questions, which she loved to do, she was never happy with the replies. Why was it that on Sundays Gaia was hardly mentioned and the service focussed exclusively on Jehallah? She had been told that it was just tradition, dating back to the time of Sh. Even as she thought about it, her forefinger went up to her lips in the time-honoured involuntary gesture. Sh. Never talk about it, try not to think about it.

Overall, though she was pretty happy at the hospital, although her parents had been disappointed that she hadn't taken up the offer of a place at The Academy to join The Elite. More than disappointed, actually, more like devastated. Her decision that her Commoner Service career should take the form of training to be a doctor had at least partially mollified them, though. They told their friends that she had always had a good heart. They weren't so pleased when she broke it to them that her field was going to be psychiatry. There were many examples of stubborn and twisted people who fought Gaia's spiritual dominance, the most extreme of whom always ended up at the hospital under psychiatric care. She was on her way now to see Gaston, who was one such case.

She made her way through the maze of hospital corridors and scowled as she nearly bumped into the gene screener as he came round a corner. He looked so superior in his Elite robes, albeit tied loosely together with a green belt denoting the humblest rank of the Elite. It made her think of her friend Zero, and she wondered how he was getting on in a life which must surely be so different from the one she had chosen. She had liked him a lot more than she had let on – he had an innocence about him which she found deeply charming. She had always been attracted to the quiet ones and she smiled inwardly at the thought of him trying to form a relationship with someone who liked to chatter as much as she did which would surely be doomed from the start!

Eventually she reached the cell in which Gaston was being held. He was, as usual, sitting in his chair looking out of the window onto the rolling hospital lawns. Someone had trussed him up in a straightjacket so that it would be safe for her to spend some time with him, although she wasn't at all frightened of him. Part of her loved him for his rebelliousness, his total refusal to accept the model of reality to which society asked him to subscribe, which he called the warp of conditioning.

She adopted her usual attitude to him, which was warm to the point of flirtatiousness.

"Gaston , darling, how are you doing today?"

He turned to look at her and smiled ruefully. He couldn't help but like the intelligent young girl to whom he had been "assigned". He looked down at his restrictive jacket.

"A bit of trust would be nice. Freedom even."

"There's no freedom under Gaia, Gaston, you know that. We all have to work together for the common good, or else suffer the pain."

"You just don't realise what's going on, none of you do. You've all bought into this Gaia crap. We all have to be goody goody and Jehallah forbid that we should think for ourselves."

Unity was polite but firm, trying as hard as she could not to sound condescending.

"The pain isn't imaginary, Gaston. We all know from birth that if we have selfish thoughts or desires which would harm humanity, Gaia punishes us with pain. We have to learn to toe the line, or else lead a miserable life. And it's good that it is this way. We all know about Sh. I know it's hard, we all fall by the wayside sometimes, but that's just how it is."

Gaston looked at her with a slightly bizarre mixture of boredom and contempt. Finally he deigned to reply.
"It's all in the mind, my lovely little conformist. We all subscribe to these notions and they become reality.

Even for me, and believe me I know how it really is, I feel the pain of selfish thinking. The warp of conditioning is so strong, we have created a reality which is so hellishly restrictive for ourselves."

"But Gaia.........." Unity started to interject.

"You still don't get it. Despite, or perhaps because of, your first class mind and education, you can't see the truth when it's staring you in the face. There's no such thing as Gaia."

7

Yearning to talk to his friend about the paper, Zero arrived early for class the next morning. He knew instinctively that the answer to the supposedly easy multiple choice question he had been posed the previous day wasn't C, but since he couldn't justify either of the other answers, he had decided to stick to his guns, and go with the obvious choice.

He was delighted to find Thomas was already sitting in the classroom, chatting to Alice. Actually, from their body language chatting up Alice would be nearer the mark.

Zero hated to cramp his friend's style but he wasn't about to sit at the back of the room and pretend he wasn't there.

"So", he began, "what's the answer to Life the Universe and Everything?"

"Good question!" Thomas turned round, his eyes shining. He wasn't about to miss a chance to show off his intellectual prowess and general knowledge in front of the girl with whom he had been flirting.

"The twentieth century writer Douglas Adams came up with the answer 'forty-two' as a humorous response to that question. He then , since his answer clearly didn't make any sense, suggested that the reason it didn't make any sense was that the question regarding the answer to 'Life, the Universe and Everything', wasn't the right question. Eventually he revealed that the correct question was 'what do you get if you multiply six by nine?'"

Alice, who looked a little as if she had been losing the thread of the conversation suddenly piped up with the obvious objection.

"But six times nine is fifty-four, surely. Why forty-two?"

Thomas was relieved that she was paying attention because what he viewed as his stroke of genius was about to be revealed.

"He was making a joke to the effect that the universe is fundamentally unlucky."

Even Zero, who normally was at least as agile mentally as his friend, was now lost. But Thomas was just warming up.

"We assume that all these numbers are to base ten. And why? Because we have ten fingers, that's why! Why should the fundamental question about the universe be affected by the number of fingers on one particular species on one particular planet orbiting one particular star? Consider the multiplication using base thirteen. Forty-two is four times thirteen plus two times one, which is fifty-four to base ten. Using base thirteen, six times nine is forty-two."

Zero had just about caught up by now. "So he was saying that the universe is actually configured to base thirteen."

"Which is a fundamentally unlucky number!" Thomas leaned back, in a rather self-satisfied way. Zero made a mental note to tell his friend that if in future he wanted to impress a girl, he should try to keep maths out of the conversation.

Their interaction was brought to an abrupt close by the entrance of the Tran. Zero couldn't help but think that this was a good thing from the point of view of his friend's amorous intentions towards Alice. He tried to put the amusing but essentially frivolous conversation out of his mind, turning his attention back to the multiple choice question set the previous day.

The class fell completely silent. That the Tran did so as well was less of a surprise after their experience the previous day. Thomas was beginning to find the Tran's mode of being irritating, and was fiddling disconsolately with his pencil. Eventually the Tran spoke.

" Time for Biology."

There was an audible groan from the class. Thomas could contain his impatience no longer.

"What about the multiple choice question? The answer to Life, The Universe and Everything! Are we just going to ignore it and move on to some Biology course?"

The Tran smiled.

"No course. There is only one Biology lesson at The Academy. Come."

The Tran stood, and walked swiftly from the classroom with his long loping gait. The class followed and were led down a long ill lit corridor into a part of the Academy they hadn't been to before. The corridor finished at the top of an old and rather rickety spiral staircase which they climbed down and down until they reached a dingy hallway from which there was only one door. On the door was a plaque, which read simply 'Biology'. Zero smiled inwardly as he recognised the Tran's distaste for excessive verbiage.

The class filed into the room which was like no classroom they had ever seen before. The walls on three sides of the room were lined with glass, which had small informative plaques. Behind two of the walls was a rather pretty wood, which they reasoned must be the small piece of woodland behind the Academy, and the third glazed wall was mostly covered by earth.

On closer inspection, the earth was actually filled with a network of tunnels, and the room had been constructed to show cavities of varying sizes. Suddenly, Zero realised that there was movement all around. Everywhere – in the earth, in the woods, in the cavities, there was a crawling mass of insect life.

Ants. An amazingly complex and orderly society was spread out before their eyes. Everywhere worker ants – wingless sterile females – were working together industriously and with an incredible degree of harmony. The soldier ants, up to ten times the size of the smallest workers, patrolled the nest and searched for food in the wood outside. Inside, there were four separate chambers for the queen, eggs, larvae and pupae. The plaques on the glass walls explained that the workers had captured the workers and brood of other species which were made to work as slaves. The colony in front of them was part of a supercolony consisting of over 300 million workers and one million queens housed in 45,000 interconnecting nests.

"Look................"

The Tran spoke as he strode towards the door. As he opened the door, with one hand resting on the handle, he turned and addressed the class again.

"............and think."

8

Over the last few days Zero had had trouble getting to sleep at night, and tonight was no exception. As his body tossed and turned on the rumpled sheets, his mind was turning over the events of the last few days. Even if he wasn't close to understanding entirely what the Tran was driving at, he was coming closer to getting to grips with the question.

How many consciousnesses are there in the universe?

The point about the 'Biology lesson' was quite clear. It wasn't possible to consider the ant colony as being made up of millions of individual consciousnesses, all interacting in such an orderly and intelligent way. No way was an ant's brain sufficiently evolved to see its place in the colony and make all the appropriate decisions, or to communicate with the other ants to the extent necessary to enable the colony to function as smoothly as it did. Zero was forced to conclude that it was the colony itself that was conscious. The individual ants had to be viewed as organs of the colony-being rather than entities in their own right. The problem was where this line of reasoning should stop. Once he had accepted the principle that consciousness doesn't necessarily rest with an individual, should the group consciousness be allocated to the colony at the Academy, or to the supercolony of 45,000 nests and one million queens?

And then there was Gaia. Clearly Gaia was a consciousness in its own right – was the Tran saying that humans were merely organs of Gaia and that their sense of being discrete consciousnesses was just illusory?

When he finally fell asleep, he had the most remarkable dream.

He was a fish, living deep in the ocean. Mostly he and his fellow members of the community of fish in the ocean depths went about their daily lives in a contented way, searching for food and looking after their fry. Every so often, though, they would wonder what their lives were all about, and contemplate the great question:

Is There an Ocean?

There were many tales of Great Fishes in the past who claimed to have *actually seen* the ocean. These Great Fishes had attracted followers who had spread the word far and wide, for they were privy to "The Knowledge", a sacred mixture of philosophy, customs and beliefs. After practicing The Knowledge in their daily lives for many years the devotees were guaranteed also to be able to see The Ocean. Temples sprung up all over the seabed, testaments to the Great Fish who had claimed to have seen The Ocean, and they were visited weekly by many of the fish who lived in that area.

When Zero awoke the following morning, he felt both disturbed and depressed. He sought out his friend, who never failed to lift his spirits.

"You're taking it all much too seriously."

Thomas leaned over and spoke softly.

"Don't forget, life is like a penis!"

Zero looked blankly at his old schoolfriend.

"The more you think about it, the harder it gets!"

They both dissolved into hysterical laughter. They chatted for a while, but Zero's thoughts started to turn to his old friend Unity, and he resolved to visit her at her hospital at the half term starting the following weekend. He hoped it wasn't Thomas's joke which had prompted the desire to see her again.

9

Unity was working the late shift and the hospital was quiet, although had Zero visited the psychiatric ward the previous week on the night of the full moon, he would have been amazed how much noisier it had been. For centuries, psychiatric wards in hospitals had been laying on extra staff on full moons to cope with the increased activity in the inmates, but today the moon was in its first quarter and the general ambience was one of dull routine.

That wasn't how it felt in Zero's stomach, however. He was amazed at how nervous he was about seeing his friend again, and even more amazed at how he felt when she turned a corner into the corridor in which he was standing and smiled at him. The warmth which started in his heart spread throughout his being and he found himself grinning stupidly.

"I brought these for you", he half stammered as he proffered the rather random assortment of flowers he had liberated from his mother's garden and formed into a rough bouquet.

Unity hugged him awkwardly and kissed him on the cheek.

"Thanks."

She looked right at him.

"You look just the same!" she exclaimed.

"Did you think the mad scientists from The Academy would have turned me into a zombie eyed clone by now?"

As soon as Zero asked the question, he realised that he had pretty much hit the nail on the head as far as she was concerned. At least his stomach was returning to normal and he was able to ask Unity some questions about her life at the hospital. She was very agitated about an astonishing new development in brain surgery shortly to be pioneered at her wing of the hospital. Using a revolutionary new technique, the surgeons reckoned it was now possible to transplant an entire brain from one human being to another, like something out of an early twentieth century horror movie. The technique also worked for substantial sections of the brain without the need to transplant the entire organ. The surgery had been tested exhaustively on apes, and the first trials on humans were due to start the following week. The intention was to take two people, one of whom was intellectually incapable of accepting the rule of Gaia and who therefore spent their lives in constant Gaia-pain, and the other of whom was well adjusted but had some debilitating physical complaint. By performing the brain transplant one of the two people would be able to lead a normal life. Gaston was to be one of the subjects for the first human trial.

"My god, it sounds like you have more than your fair share of mad scientists here!" Zero was appalled, of course, but he couldn't help himself from also wondering about the philosophical implications.

"Do you realise what this means?" He was reeling from the questions posed by this.

Unity almost snapped at him. "Of course I do. It means a human being is being created from the waste parts of two people. It means someone is being subjected to a life of physical and mental anguish, mitigated only by constant morphine injections. It means the doctors here have abandoned any pretence at humanity. It means there's no bloody hope for the human race."

She started to cry, and Zero put his arms round her in an attempt to comfort her. He was by now deeply ashamed of his line of thought but he couldn't stop himself from expressing his query.

"Gaston", he said, and Unity pulled back from his embrace and looked at him.

"I mean, if Gaston is forced into this, and the experiment is a success........."

Unity suddenly realised what he was getting at. "Who will he be when the experiment is over? Will he be in physical and mental anguish, or in his own body with a new brain?"

"Exactly. Nobody knows for sure, of course, because the experiment has never been done before, but most people would probably suppose that Gaston would find himself in the disabled body. But does the sense of individual consciousness attach itself to the brain or to the body? And if it does attach itself to the brain, to which part? Suppose they transplant only some of the brain. Where would Gaston end up then?" Zero realised that Unity was crying again, and once again put his arms round her. This time she pulled back, unwilling to let him comfort her.

"Bloody typical man! I've just told you about a proposed act of mindless butchery and you want to talk philosophy. It's like your stupid question you used to discuss with Thomas."

Zero had forgotten about the question which had obsessed the two friends some years before. Thomas had posed the question 'If you had the opportunity now of having electrodes implanted in your brain which ensured that you would have no more Gaia-pain and would also be blissful for the rest of your life, would you take it?' Thomas maintained that it would be illogical not to take such an opportunity but Zero was repelled by the idea. He reckoned that human beings needed to live through a variety of emotions and sensations for their lives to have meaning, and the two of them had argued their opposing cases for months. Surprisingly, every single person who they asked agreed with Zero – the revulsion for the idea in their classmates was unanimous.

Sometimes Zero felt that his compulsion to wonder what life was all about was a severe handicap, and this was one of those moments. He apologised profusely to Unity, who seemed to accept the apology. They spent another hour comparing their lives since they had both left school. Unity told him all about her life at the hospital, and about her friendship with Gaston the gatheist. Zero had never heard of a gatheist before – how could someone not believe in Gaia when every selfish thought or action was rewarded with Gaia-pain? He was also fascinated by the gene screeners and promised to try to find out more about their function when he returned to the Academy after half term. They parted on very friendly terms, vowing to meet again soon.

10

Returning to the Academy after half term was a real joy. It was great for Zero to see his friends again, and he had missed the intellectual challenges. Home had become a pretty dull place. He was even more excited to discover that they would be studying the history of Chrislam with Paul. The only fly in the ointment was that he recalled that they were required to study Consciousness before learning about the early days of Chrislam and the dawn of the Age of Gaia, and he wasn't at all sure how much progress he had made down that road. He had spent much of the half term lying on his bed staring at the ceiling and trying to make sense of his lessons with the Tran. It was clear that they were being told that the notion that consciousness attaches to an individual in a way which is discrete from the rest of reality is illusory. Somehow, everyone is connected to Gaia in some way but how Gaia, Jehallah and an individual are related hardly seemed to be explained by a roomful of ants.

Paul was his usual friendly self and was clearly delighted to see his students again. He asked a few twinkly eyed knowing questions about how they had got on with the Tran, and then announced that they were now ready to start learning about the early days of Chrislam. He started by asking if they had any questions. Laurence, a dark skinned quiet boy with greasy hair, immediately put up his hand.

"Please could you tell us about the time of Sh." He put his finger to his lips, and glanced furtively around the classroom.

Every child with two neurons to rub together had wondered about this, but it had always been made clear that they weren't allowed even to ask the question.

Paul's reaction was slightly unexpected – he doubled up and howled and howled with laughter, his body shaking uncontrollably. Eventually he stood up and spoke, tears still running down his cheeks.

"Sorry. That always gets me. Sh stands for secular humanism. We can talk about it all you like. It's a belief system particularly prevalent in so-called civilised countries in pre-Gaia times which combines a belief in the necessity to be kind to people with a lack of belief in the existence of Jehallah."

The class gasped at the latter concept. How was it possible for people not to believe in Jehallah?

"It's not as strange as it sounds. Even now, when we know that Gaia will punish selfish thoughts with Gaia-pain, there are still people who don't believe in Gaia. We call them gatheists, and they have to be treated in a psychiatric hospital because they are more or less permanently subject to Gaia-pain. Before the dawn of the age of Gaia, people were free to think whatever they wanted. Nowadays of course even to think about the possibility that we are all separate and independent of Gaia and Jehallah causes so much Gaia-pain that it has been accepted that we don't talk about secular humanism at all. Except here, of course..."

Thomas couldn't prevent himself from butting in.

"So the initials of secular humanism conveniently mean to be quiet. But why can we talk about it here? We've all talked about this a lot – we have all experienced virtually no Gaia-pain since we joined the Academy. It's like the laws of the universe don't apply to us any more."

Paul was quiet for quite a while. Eventually he addressed the question.

"There are various ways of looking at this and none of them are quite right, because it is impossible for our minds to grasp who or what Gaia is exactly. If we say for the sake of argument that Gaia is the Earth spirit, the consciousness which flows through all the Earth's inhabitants, and then pretend that Gaia is an individual, just on a bigger scale, then I could answer your question by saying that *Gaia wants Academy students to know and understand more*. Like the ant colony, humans have been divided by Gaia into castes – commoners, carers and the Elite here at the Academies. There is another caste too. Our roles as Elite members and trainees necessitates a higher level of understanding which most people simply aren't equipped to cope with – they have to be controlled by Gaia for the common good. You are all the lucky ones, who have escaped a life subject to the tyranny of Gaia-pain."

Like the rest of the class, Zero felt that Paul's talk had raised at least as many questions as it answered.

"So why were we chosen? Was it just on the basis of academic ability? And how did Gaia come into existence? How can it be that there was a time when Gaia *wasn't there*, and then a time when she *was*?"

"Your first questions will be dealt with later on. The question of how Gaia came into existence is fascinating of course, and the truth is that nobody really knows the answer. It seems that Gaia has always been in existence but her control over humanity is relatively recent. As to what prompted the amazing transformation, we can only really speculate. There was a period after the merging of Christianity and Islam when the world seemed to come closer together – individual cultures lost their integrity and blurred together. Advances in technology enabled people to remain in ever closer contact. The Consciousness of Gaia had always flowed through every human on the planet but it seems that a combination of circumstances conspired to break down the individual's illusion of separateness to the extent that Gaia was able to exert more direct control over the thoughts and behaviour of individuals. At first, of course, nobody knew what was happening – you can imagine the confusion, and initially the Gaia-pain was sporadic as well as unexplained. Once the realisation that it was Gaia the Earth spirit who was taking more control over the thoughts and behaviour of humans took hold, the grip of Gaia became total. A shared belief is a very powerful thing, much more so than we realise."

Of the fourteen thousand remaining questions Zero wanted to ask, one was the most pressing.

"But what about Jehallah and Botu? Where do they come into all this?"

"To answer this question you need to know a little more about the history of religion. In pre-Chrislamic times, Christianity and Islam weren't the only religions. Two of the other main world faiths, Hinduism and Buddhism, had a more detached and, some would say, introspective, approach to spirituality. Indeed, Buddhism did not even admit the existence of God in the sense that we might understand it, but rather taught a path by which individuals could come to realise their *Buddha-nature*, which was a state of oneness with universal consciousness which was perceived to be ones true self, and the birthright of every human being. Many of the practices of both Hindus and Buddhists involved the transcending of the perceived material world. Around the same time as Christianity and Islam fused into Chrislam, the other more introspective religions fused into one group, who called themselves Transcendentalists."

Zero realised what Paul was saying at about the same time as the rest of his class, but verbalised it first.

"Trans!"

"Of course. But whereas the Christian emphasis had always been on the relationship between the individual and Jehovah, or Allah in the case of Muslims, or Jehallah after the two merged, the Buddhist approach in particular was more impersonal. They needed a phrase to express what they perceived to be the conscious energy which flows through the universe, and Buddha-nature wasn't impartial enough for the Hindus or the other transcendentalist religions. Eventually they settled on the rather unwieldy *bliss of the universe.*"

Again Zero was incapable of preventing himself from interjecting.

"Botu!"

Paul smiled indulgently.

"You'll have to try and stop yourself from stating the obvious. It's a bad habit."

"But why haven't these two names and approaches merged? Why continue to have both Botu and Jehallah?"

"Because there is a very real difference in both belief and approach. The Chrislamic doctrine is that there is a universal consciousness, Jehallah, with whom we can have a relationship, but the trans go further and state that the bliss of the universe, Botu, is our real nature. These two approaches can't be reconciled."

"And where does Gaia come into all this?"

Paul threw back his head and laughed.

"Too many questions for one lesson. And besides, I have another test for you. I know how you all enjoyed the first one!"

It had seemed a long time since they had all been asked to "write all you know".

"Don't worry. This test doesn't just consist of one question."

Paul's eyes twinkled as he handed out the test papers. Zero wondered why it was that even the best teachers seemed to take pleasure in their charges' discomfort. Eventually, after what seemed an age, they were allowed to turn over their papers.

Once again, there was a simple header across the top of the page, this time stating simply "Academy Examination 0/2". And as Paul had said there was more than one question. In fact there were two:

1. "Who am I?"
2. "What is life?"

11

Once again, Zero had that feeling that Unity's choice of life in the hospital had some merit, compared to these ridiculous questions The Academy kept flinging at them. His mind reeled with a sense of panic – how could he possibly be expected to answer these questions? They had been allowed only half an hour, and given six sheets of paper, when great men throughout history had devoted their lives to these very issues and in some cases had seemingly made no progress whatsoever.

Eventually, his mind calmed down. He recalled that these were the questions at the beginning of chapter one of the "Academy Consciousness Course", and also that they weren't exactly answered in the printout they had been given. Eventually, he found himself settling into the state he had experienced when he was with the Tran, of calm alertness. These were not questions to which there were definite answers. All he could do was to express his understanding so far.

All of his experiences at The Academy – the lessons, the ants and particularly the long silences with the Tran, had begun to give him the feeling that there was indeed one consciousness which flows throughout everything in creation, at the basis of his being and of every other being in the cosmos. But he couldn't think of a way of expressing that on paper without reducing the answers to dry intellectualisations of what was in effect ultimate truth, if indeed there was such a thing.

Suddenly he had a flash of inspiration, and wrote two short sentences, one of 11 words, the other of 13. As he handed in his answer after only some ten minutes, he was aware of the wry resentment of his classmates, still madly scribbling, and a grin from Thomas in friendly recognition of what he assumed was another burst of clarity from his friend. Zero made to leave, but was stopped by Paul, who explained that there was another chapter of the Academy Consciousness Course to be handed out at the end of the test, and he was made to return to his seat. He didn't particularly enjoy the time, most of which he spent wondering whether or not he would be kicked out for barefaced cheek. He had got away with a glib answer to the previous test but perhaps he shouldn't make a habit of it.

Paul, meanwhile, took a surreptitious look at Zero's answer, and was delighted by what he saw. The paper in front of him read:

The answer to neither of these questions can be written down.

All that can be said is that both questions have the same answer.

A few minutes later, Paul collected the remaining scripts and handed out the next instalment of the Academy course to the rather shocked looking students. This was about the stage of the year when it became clear that some of the class weren't quite up to the rigours of the course, and they would be rescheduled into less demanding curricula. Obviously, though, there were several members who were destined to rise to the very top of the Academy Elite.

Later that evening, Zero spent some time contemplating his answer, with the result that he became increasingly pleased with himself. The more he thought about it, the more he came to the conclusion that the two questions in the test should not be answered directly. It was some time, therefore, before he got around to opening the sheet handed to him by Paul. He remembered the informal humour of the first chapter, and although he was tired, he couldn't resist a peek at the second one. This was much shorter, and written in a very different form, without paragraphs:

Academy Consciousness Course
Chapter Two

Can we imagine a world without life? Unless you believe that everything in the universe is purely mechanical, then we can certainly say that *life exists*. Many people throughout the ages have believed that there is no such thing as life, and we live in a clockwork universe with consciousness simply an illusionary phenomenon, but nowadays in the Age of Gaia such a belief is rare. Granted, it is hard or even impossible to be sure, but we can assume for the sake of this course that the answer A to the question posed in Chapter one, that there are no consciousnesses in the universe, is invalid. Really it should be coming clearer and clearer to the student that there is only one consciousness which flows throughout everything and everyone. All things in creation have the life force flowing through them, and whether or not we say something is *alive* simply reflects whether or not that object appears to respond to the life force, the one consciousness. Nothing is immune to this force, things just react differently. Over centuries, even rocks which at first sight seem totally inert, will weather away, and indeed on an atomic level they are overflowing with energy and dynamism, plants are able to react more to the life force so we say they are *alive*, animals react more still, humans more and, it must be said, some humans more than others. Such is the beauty of creation that there are clues embedded within it which point towards this truth, that consciousness is universal and not restricted as might first appear to us, to individuals. Ants, for example, are one such clue as it is clear that the ant colony is better perceived as the unit of consciousness than the individual ant. Like acrostics, where the first letter of each sentence in a chapter, or the first letter of each chapter in a book, spells out a hidden message, so there are such clues hidden within creation. If you are attentive throughout your life, these clues will become clear, and the consciousness present, hidden behind the world of form, will become apparent to you. Self, behind who you think you are, is actually omnipresent, and is the Self of all things.

Zero found this immensely elevating, and had a strange feeling that he was entering into a new stage of his quest for knowledge, but before he could contemplate this short chapter more, he fell asleep, and the paper fell from his hand to the floor.

12

Without any kind of greeting Thomas, clearly brimming with excitement, practically launched himself at Zero when they met the next day in class.

"What do you think? What does it mean?"

Zero agreed that it was a challenging piece of philosophy, but made some comment to the effect that it was pretty much a continuation of the line of thought on which the course had been taking them since the beginning.

Thomas was clearly surprised by his friend's reaction, and then the reality dawned.

"You're not telling me you didn't notice."

Zero looked blank, and Thomas started to laugh.

"You didn't even notice the acrostic, did you. Mr Clever Clogs all-that-can-be-said-is-that-both-questions-have-the-same-answer missed the entire point! Not that I'm entirely sure what that point is, mind you."

Thomas pulled out the paper they had all been handed out the day before. In pencil he had underlined the first letters of each sentence.

"It was a pretty broad hint, that bit about the first letters of each sentence in a chapter or the first letter of each chapter in a book containing a hidden message. Look!"

The underlined letters read CUMGRANOSALIS.

"Cum grano salis" Zero read out aloud.

"But what does it mean?"

"It means 'with a grain of salt'", Zero pointed out helpfully.

"I know that, dumbass. We did Latin together, remember? I mean why should such a serious point have such a frivolous hidden meaning?"

"Beats me." Zero was feeling a little embarrassed about having missed at least part of the point of the script. If he was honest with himself, he was also growing slightly weary of the whole Academy experience. He had always been driven to understand what was going on around him, but the course on which he had embarked never seemed to provide answers, only more and more questions.

This brief spell of uncharacteristic melancholy was broken when the door to the classroom opened and the Tran walked in. Zero was filled by the now familiar sense of the compelling presence of the man, and he found himself sinking into a deep sense of peace. Then, with a sweet and lilting voice, the Tran began to sing:

"No pleasure, no pain, can affect my true Self.
Both suffering and pleasure belong to the mind.
The Self is the witness of all the mind's play
Remaining forever conscious and free.

The Self, like an object reflected in glass
Appears to be mind and the whole universe.
And man by forgetting his identity
Is lost in delusion and knows misery.

All teachings of sages have one common goal:
They all teach the way to attain self-control.
The highest religion consists of just this:
To bridle the mind and in truth become fixed.

The uncontrolled mind is man's sole evil foe.
It vanquishes men with its weapons of woe.
Forgetful of this, men see evil in men,
Like fools they forget that all evil's within.

None other can cause me to know joy or pain
For I am forever the unchanging One.
The sense of delight or of sadness, I find,
Comes from the false notion that I am the mind.

The body and mind are both subject to change
But I am the one in whom all is contained.
In freedom forever, beyond shame or fear
The sweet blissful Self is the One I hold dear."

Listening to the song, Zero felt himself becoming clearer and clearer, more and more expanded, until all sensory and experiential boundaries had been dissolved. He was Zero, he was the Tran, he was everywhere and in everything. He was Light, Love, pure Bliss beyond imagining.

And at last he knew. He knew why the understanding that there is only one consciousness had to be taken with a grain of salt. He knew why The Academy taught the way it did, with question after question. He knew about Jehallah and Botu. He knew about Gaia. And he knew what he had to do.

13

Nine months had passed since Zero had left The Academy. Leaving had been easy, but there was no shortage of people telling him he was being a fool.

First the Tran, explaining to him that Trans were the fourth and highest caste, able to explore the depths of bliss within themselves, and to radiate peace and harmony to the ignorant around them, people who were unaware of their true nature and were closer to the vegetable kingdom than to the heights of humanity which were being scaled by the Trans. Zero was now ready to become a Tran. Commoners and Carers thought that Academy members were The Elite, but Trans were the real elite, formed from the cream of Academy students. But Zero had already thought about this years before, when he used to debate with Thomas whether or not they would accept electrodes planted in their brain to eliminate Gaia-pain and be blissful for the rest of their life. He knew that the life of a Tran, noble tradition though it might be, was not for him.

He had then been honoured to receive a visit from Seven, the Academy President. Seven had explained that Zero was a Single Digit, selected by the gene screeners at birth for high office, based on his genome printout. The genes responsible for the ability to transcend Gaia and rule with wisdom had been known for some time, and the tradition had grown for gene screeners to instruct parents to name such children with a single digit – Zero, Unity, Two, Three, Four, Five, Six, Seven,

Eight or Nine. After that, there was no guarantee that Single Digits would fulfil their potential, but many rose to high office within the Academy. Zero, of course, thought of Unity, who had chosen the path of Carer instead. Zero's genome printout had been exceptional, scoring in the top 0.00001% for intelligence and with higher scores for clarity, intuition and insight than had ever previously been recorded. The Academy had been keeping an even closer eye than usual on him, and it was entirely likely that he would be offered the job of President when Seven retired in a few years. The Trans, he claimed, were only the self-proclaimed pinnacles of human evolution. There was no higher calling than to be Academy President, to shape the way society evolved to an extent which was unprecedented in human history. But Zero couldn't see himself in office, constrained by governmental duties and regulations. His plan was clear, and he had resolved to put it into action the next day.

Unity had been in a terrible state when he turned up at the hospital. Gaston's surgery had taken place just two days before, and she was overcome with anger and grief. Zero didn't dare ask the philosophical question which had been plaguing him, as he was certain he would become the object of her anger if he did. As it happened, he didn't need to, as she blurted it all out.

"Gaston is now in the body of a man suffering from motor neurone disease. He can hardly speak at the best of times, and anyway he is constantly doped up to the eyeballs on morphine. They have thrown him away. By putting what they think of as a sick mind in what they think of as a sick body they feel they have done no wrong. Instead, there was a party last night to celebrate the creation of a "whole human being", the man created with the other mind and Gaston's body, who they feel will be able to take his place in society. At the same time, they have answered your question – the sense of self goes with the mind and not the body."

She started sobbing uncontrollably and Zero put his arms round her.

"At least its all over now", he said as soothingly as he could.

She pulled away violently.

"But it's not! It's only the beginning! They have started to wonder with which part of the mind the human is identified. The common assumption is that the sense of self is carried with the memory, and they have found an amnesiac to play with to see what happens when his mind is transferred into another body. It's just unspeakable. To think that I entered this profession to try to help people. What am I going to do Zero?"

And she fell back into his arms sobbing.

" I actually came here today to ask you out. I would really like to spend more time with you and wondered if you would like to have dinner with me some time?"

Zero had pictured himself asking the question many times on the way over to the hospital but he hadn't anticipated her state and was wondering if he should have waited.

Unity was thrilled to accept, though. She kissed him on the cheek.

"Jehallah bless you, Zero, I would love to."

And so it was that Zero turned his back on the life of a Tran and the life of an Academy Elite Member and chose instead the path of the heart. They would go for long walks in the meadows near where she lived, where at first they held hands, and later on they made love. She taught him how to please her and they led a happy carefree existence. Unity would work at the hospital, caring as best she could for the patients and campaigning against the mindswap experiments until eventually they were stopped. Eventually Zero moved in with her and performed what was traditionally the role of the wife, baking bread, cooking and looking after the house. It was without doubt the happiest time in both of their lives.

14

Meandering past the valley where they used to walk was a crystal clear stream. Zero loved to sit by the stream, sometimes for hours at a time, marvelling at its beauty, delighting in its sound, and wondering at the myriad of life forms which made it their home.

At one point, around an hour's walk from their cottage, the stream formed a pond where there was an old mill with a millwheel which was still functioning, turning lazily and apparently effortlessly.

This was Zero's absolutely favourite spot, and he and Unity were lying together on the bank one sunny summer afternoon. They had just made love, and the warm glow of sun on their skins matched perfectly the glow they each felt inside of love for one another. Unity was playing with a blade of grass, holding it in her hand and watching the gentle breeze bend it to and fro. Zero was looking at the mill.

Unity, in that way that lovers have, immediately picked up a change in Zero's mood, a slight raising in intensity.

"What are you thinking, handsome?" She smiled, and rolled over so she could look right at him.

"Just looking at the windmill"

"I know you, you're thinking something. Worse than that, you're not thinking about me anymore, you're off somewhere." She prodded him playfully in the ribs.

"The windmill. It doesn't know about the stream."

"Of course it doesn't, silly, it's a pile of bricks. Honestly, you could get all philosophical about anything, an ant or an earthworm."

"Actually ants are very interesting......." He stopped himself when he saw the look on her face. This wasn't the time to discuss the consciousness of a colony.

"Anyway, what do you mean about the windmill?" Her curiosity had been roused.

"Well obviously windmills can't think, but if they could, they wouldn't know about the stream. I mean I bet they would think that the energy required for the wheel to turn was their own."

Unity was no intellectual slouch, she had after all been classified as a "single digit" by the Academy.

"You are drawing an analogy with humans. They mistakenly believe themselves to be separate discrete organisms and are unaware that consciousness is a universal phenomenon which flows through everything and everyone, giving life to any organism sufficiently complex to respond to it."

"I love it when you talk dirty."

They both laughed.

"But I wouldn't say that consciousness gives life. *Consciousness is life.* The universe is alive. Life flows through everything............."

He paused and looked briefly disconsolate.

"Words are so inadequate. As soon as you try to say something, somehow the truth has slipped through between the gaps. The words are always too clumsy, too gross, too worldly. When I left the Academy I was determined to share some of the Elite's knowledge with the world, but it's so difficult....."

"Difficult, or impossible?" She smiled at him with a glint of mischief. She knew what she was doing. She was challenging him. She also knew he could never resist a challenge.

"You're right!" He sat up straight and became very animated.

"That's what I have to do! I left The Academy to do it and I must find a way......." His voice trailed off as he started to think about his new project.

Unity smiled. Since time immemorial, wives have been gently guiding their husbands in the direction they would like them to go. And since time immemorial husbands have been almost completely unaware of the process.

Zero was lost to the world now, his mind racing with ideas. How could he possibly express all that he knew. It really was the "write all you know challenge" all over again, except this time a glib answer wouldn't be acceptable.

Unity rolled back onto her back, and watched the sunlight playing through the leaves of the trees. Once again, the breeze caressed the blade of grass in her hand. She was happy, happier than she had ever been.

15

It had been some time since Zero had last seen Thomas. He knew that Thomas had elected to stay at the Academy and that his career there had been successful. Although not a "single digit" (he was told that his genome denoted a mind which although razor sharp, was too *linear* to qualify for that ranking), his abilities had been recognized and he was now black belted and already teaching courses to the new students.

At the knock at the door, Zero jumped up and rushed to open it. He knew it would be good to see his old friend again but it was more than that, it was absolutely wonderful. There is nothing in this world quite like an old childhood friend.

They embraced, and Zero was surprised to find tears welling in his eyes at the sheer joy of the reunion. When he drew back and looked long and hard at Thomas, it was as though nothing had changed, they had never been apart.

Zero suggested a walk, and they wandered along the path by the stream, Zero delighting in sharing his favourite places with his old companion. They talked and talked, and Zero delighted in his friend's success and obvious pleasure in Academy life. Thomas made a point of stressing that Zero was much talked about and that a place would be found for him at the Academy whenever he wanted to go back. This was the first slightly awkward moment as Zero was sure he didn't want to return, and wasn't quite sure how to tell his friend without hurting his feelings.

Eventually, Thomas rather hesitantly asked what Zero was doing with his life. He was evidently unimpressed by a description of a day involving bread baking and long walks, and enquired further about the direction in which Zero wanted his life to go. Zero had decided not to talk about his writing project, but finally agreed to show Thomas some of it when they returned to the cottage.

Later, by a log fire and over a cup of tea, Thomas was presented with the first draft of Zero's pamphlet. He picked it up, and held it in his hand, weighing it as if it were a bag of fruit or vegetables.

"This is the sum total of all your knowledge?"

"Yup".

"Bit short, isn't it?"

Zero laughed, for there was no malice in the remark, which was clearly meant humorously.

Thomas started to read a section, but soon afterwards found himself shaking his head. He reread the section out loud.

"The Universe is conscious. The act of calling that consciousness "God" is an act of rejection, forcing an estrangement. We are creating something or someone to yearn for when both we and the yearning are shallow fiction. The yearning is that moment's manifestation of the object of yearning itself (consciousness) distorted by the warp of conditioning. Consciousness flows through us and is twisted into yearning by our skin-encapsulated ego.

That the object of our yearning is the same as the source of our being is absurd, although perhaps no less absurd than any other form of desire.

To know this, and also to feel 'The drunkenness of things being various' is the glory of creation".

"Zero, my dear old friend, can I ask you a question?"

"Of course", Zero replied with a growing sense of apprehension.

"Just who is this book of yours written for?"

"It's written for everyone, not just Academy members." Zero's defensiveness was beginning to make him slightly aggressive.

"Zero, most people think of God, or Jehallah, as a white bearded old man who lives in some sort of mezzanine floor above the clouds, and is subject to violent mood swings. Your philosophical musings about the disadvantages of thinking of the Universal Consciousness as God are going to fall on deaf ears I'm afraid."

"Perhaps you have been in the Academy too long, my friend. I don't hold such an elitist world view. I believe that every person in the world has spiritual depth and many people would enjoy reading such a book"

Zero was by now leaving the trenches of his defensive position and was searching around for verbal trebuchets with which to assault the castle of his old friend's position. Thomas, however, was having none of it.

"And have you come up with a title for this world shattering epic?" Thomas enquired.

"I have been thinking along the lines of 'Towards a Nested Theory of Consciousness'".

"Snappy. The idea being..."

"The idea being essentially that Consciousness is a universal phenomenon which flows through everything. If a system is sufficiently complex, it seems to be alive and it perceives itself to be alive. But further than this, a very complex system can perceive itself to be alive, *and can contain subsystems which also perceive themselves to be alive.* Gaia is the obvious example. Gaia is a conscious being, but we are now all part of Gaia and at the same time conscious beings ourselves. Similarly the ant colony is a conscious being, as is an individual ant within it. As we learned in the Academy, different beings are more or less conscious, but in every case consciousness itself is not their own, but is the Universal Consciousness flowing through them. The apparent paradox of the nested quality of consciousness in Gaia and in the ant colony can only be explained by attributing consciousness itself to the Universal Consciousness."

"And Jehallah?"

"Is a word for Universal Consciousness. The advantage of naming it Jehallah is that we can more easily form a relationship with it as we would with another human, the disadvantage is that it denies the ultimate reality that at the core of our being we are ourselves Universal Consciousness."

Thomas was silent for some time.

"I would be careful about talking about Jehallah like that. You had better have a pretty strong lock on your door if you are going to try to publish something which might be derogatory to Someone so cherished."

Zero realised that his friend was right. He had known at The Academy after the Tran had sung his song what he had to do, which was to marry Unity and to try to write down everything he knew, to actually fulfil the challenge set to him when he had first joined The Academy and to share this knowledge beyond the walls of The Academy, but this was not the way to go about it. Nobody was ever going to read such dry ramblings and even if they did they were likely to be offended by his remarks about Jehallah. He was going to have to start from scratch.

But even as he realised this, the solution came to him. He bid his friend a fond farewell and sat down to write.

16

New thoughts seemed to come much more easily to Zero than to most people and it only took a week or so for the new book to come pouring onto the vellum on which he was writing.

He wanted Unity to see the manuscript first, and they settled down one evening by the fire for her to read it. She looked at him, knowing how much it meant to him and apprehensive about starting to read it. What if she didn't like it? Her fears dissolved quickly, as she realised just how familiar the book was to her. The first page started as follows:

"Mindful immediately of the significance of the day, Zero sat bolt upright in bed, instantly wide awake. He was full of calm, coherent energy, his mind stilled and made powerful by the awareness that today heralded the start of a period of great personal evolution, perhaps even escape from the grip of Gaia.

He remained in a state of bliss while his body dressed itself rapidly and rushed down the stairs, to be greeted by his mother proffering an earthenware bowl filled with rice. He started to eat greedily, without attention, and immediately (even more sharply than usual) experienced Gaia's rebuke. His face displayed the habitual grimace, and he silenced himself inwardly for a moment of gratitude, and ate the remainder of his breakfast with the long-practised reverential attitude which would ensure no more Gaia-pain. He kissed his mother and hugged her, knowing that he wouldn't see her again for several months then grabbed his coat, flew through the door and mounted his bicycle in what felt like one fluid movement."

Unity stopped reading and looked up.

"This is *your* story. The story of your life!"

"Actually its ours. And I want to dedicate it to you. How do you thank someone who has given their life to you? You can't, of course, but maybe this is a start...... my start anyway."

"And also it seems relevant to the themes of the book. After all, none of us are who we think we are. We just make up an idea of who we are as we go along. In a sense, we are all writing our own story."

Unity looked at him and smiled.

"I like it better than the last version. Is it finished?"

"Not quite. I have one final idea which rather turns the whole thing upside down. I have spent so much of my life searching for meaning in life, and I have come to the conclusion that I have been looking in entirely the wrong way, or at least from the wrong place."

"The wrong place?"

"I have been looking with my head! If you spend your life analysing everything, you eventually are forced to the conclusion that the world has no meaning, despite all its beauty. But if you look with your heart, suddenly everything you see is soaked in meaning. Meaning is everywhere."

Unity just smiled at him.

"I'm a woman, love. We've known that all along."

17

Don't imagine, dear reader, that this little story is quite over.

For one thing, keen students of chapter acrostics will have deduced that there is at least one more chapter to go, and that it begins with a "D".

And of course, in life there are no beginnings and no endings. Indeed, the story of Zero and Unity in many ways forms the beginning of a much bigger story, still to be told.

A month or so after Unity had first read Zero's manuscript, Thomas managed to take some time off his increasingly busy Academy schedule, and the three friends found themselves sitting by the river bank next to the old mill which Zero loved so much.

From Zero's point of view, everything was much as it had always been, except that he found himself increasingly filled with a deep sense of joy on a day to day basis. He looked at his two companions bathed in afternoon sunshine and was overwhelmed by an awareness of a quietness which filled his mind and heart and which seemed to reach out throughout time and space. He found himself laughing quietly to himself at his earnest search for truth as young man, as if truth was some formula to be deduced from the available data.

But everything was not quite as it had always been.

The gene screeners had known, for some time, of this possibility. There was no way of telling for sure, of course, there were too many possible genetic variations. But this was the current hot topic at the Academy genetics department. Theses had been written assessing the probability of this event. They had the map of Zero's genome which was of course remarkable and in an idle moment so typical of great academic discovery, a gene screener had matched it to the map of Unity's genome. Some of the possible matches were so far outside their experience that they could only begin to wonder at the being who might be produced from such a union. Or, the offspring could be quite ordinary, there was no way of telling.

And yet it had come to pass. Just as Zero was enjoying his afternoon on the riverbank with his friends, so there was growing in Unity a being so exceptional in every way, so much more luminous than any who had gone before, that the world would never be the same again.

The Age of Gaia was nearly at an end.

If you have enjoyed Age of Gaia, here is the first chapter from the next book in the Gaia trilogy Avatar of Gaia to be published shortly.

1

"You just can't do that! You're flying in the face of the whole tradition!"

Albert was working himself into a rage. The life of a gene screener contained little excitement and tended to attract individuals who were quiet to the point of nerdishness. But this really was unprecedented and Albert took his duties seriously. Worse still, it was beginning to look like he was losing the battle. And there weren't many battles in the life of what was essentially a genetic librarian, so it would be a while before he had another chance to win one.

Felicity had taken it upon herself to act as a spokesperson for the rest.

"But this is a completely unprecedented situation. We have talked about a PG for years but never really dreamed it would ever happen. And here it is, a perfect genome, and a single digit just won't do it. To use a universal constant is the only way to mark the event. We have to call him i, pi, c or e. The numbers around which the universal equations revolve. What could be more appropriate?"

Albert did his very best to calm down. He could see that he wasn't going to win the argument and he had just thought of a way to salvage some pride. If he couldn't maintain the tradition, at least he might be able to choose the name.

"You can't call him c, that's just plain daft. If you call him i his whole life will sound like that terrible character Ja-Ja Binks from the dreadful Star Wars movie. 'I's going to play football next term'. You've got the same problem with e, except his life will sound like Dick Van Dyke in Mary Poppins. We'll call him Pi, but against my better judgement."

The others looked at each other. It had been something of an effort to go through this controversy and they were looking forward to returning to a life of calculations and undisturbed analysis. Felicity took her final opportunity to speak for the rest.

"Pi it is then."

Having settled their rare contretemps they were able to refocus on the wonder of the event which was about to take place. The boy was going to be a perfect human being, an unblemished reflection of The Absolute. Of course there were stories about it having happened before, but never without a major new religion being formed around the individual concerned.

"The attraction between the parents must have been colossal."

Albert was back to a more philosophical frame of mind.

Frank, a tall bespectacled young gene screener with a slightly nervous disposition was able to concur.

"Apparently the father was going to be offered the job of Academy President, but turned it down. Just dropped out, and has never been seen since."

"Gaia wouldn't have given him a choice. This child had to be born. Of course, the father wouldn't have known why he was doing it, other than for the love of the mother. He could have thought he was dropping out for any number of reasons."

The gene screeners knew that when people thought they were making a choice like that, they were simply confused. People didn't choose the thoughts which came to them. To see the genetic evolution over the last hundred years was to see the mind of Gaia. And all of that process led to a single point. Right here and now.

Pi.